Harpo

The Baby Harp Seal

By Patricia Arrigoni

Photographs by
Patricia Arrigoni, Fred Bruemmer, David White,
and the International Fund for Animal Welfare

Travel Publishers International

To
Brian Davies
and
the International Fund for Animal Welfare
who saved the baby harp seals from
mass commercial slaughter
and to
Fred Bruemmer
whose magnificent books
The Life of the Harp Seal
and
Seasons of the Seal
told the world about them.

Published by Travel Publishers International,
Post Office Box 1030, Fairfax, California 94978.

Telephone: 800-9-HARPO-0 (800-942-7760)

Printed in the United States.

Library of Congress Catalog Number: 94–090107
ISBN: 0–9625468–8–7

Photo Credits

Patricia Arrigoni: Pages 1, 3, 5, 6, 7, 10, 11, 15, 20, 21, 22, 25, 26, 28, 31, 32, and jacket photos of Fred Bruemmer and David White
Fred Bruemmer: Pages 12, 13, 18, 24, 27, and jacket photo of Patricia Arrigoni
International Fund for Animal Welfare: Pages 8, 9, 23
IFAW/David White: Pages 4, 14, 16–17, 19, 30, and jacket photo of Brian Davies
Cover photograph: Fred Bruemmer

Acknowledgments

A special thanks to Mr. and Mrs. Stephen Lyons of Gwent, Wales, who gave us permission to print the photographs of their daughter, Sarah, on pages 17 and 19 (duplicate on back cover). Thanks also to Brian Davies, who is pictured on pages 16, 21, and 30.

Production Credits

Copyediting: Linda Falken
Text and cover design: Janet Durey Bollow
Map: Glen Dines
Separations: Repro-Media, San Francisco, California

Disclaimer: The purpose of this book is to educate and entertain. The author and Travel Publishers International shall have neither liability nor responsibility to any person or entity with respect to any loss or damage caused or alleged to be caused, directly or indirectly, by information contained in this book.

Introduction

For ages, the late winter sea ice off the coast of eastern Canada has turned into a glorious wildlife nursery with the birth of hundreds of thousands of white-coated harp seal pups. But for centuries, drifting with the winds and currents, the baby seals have been found and killed by people.

I still remember the first baby seal I saw killed. It was March, 1966. The animal was a little ball of white fur with big dark eyes. Just like Harpo in this wonderful little book,

he was only ten days old. Playfully, he went to greet the first person he had ever seen and was, by that same person, clubbed to death.

The campaign to save the baby seals involved caring children everywhere. Eventually it turned the world against the seal hunt, and the commercial slaughter of whitecoat pups was stopped in Canada. Harmless seal watching tours have now replaced the hunt.

Brian Davies
Founder
International Fund for
Animal Welfare (IFAW)

3

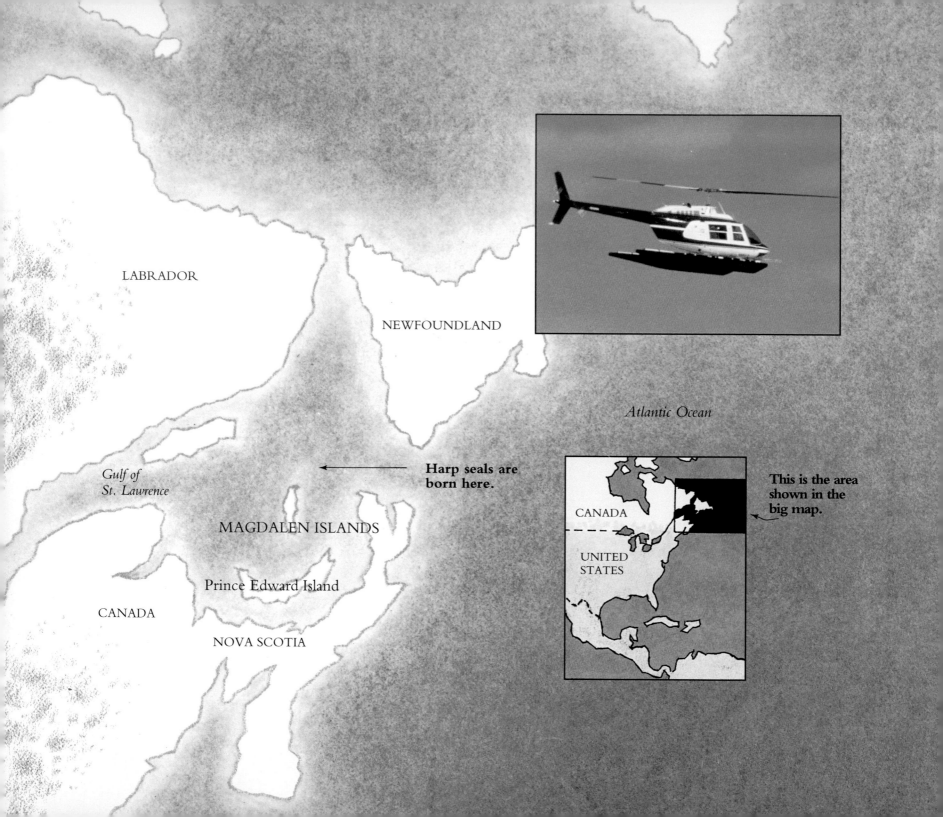

LABRADOR

NEWFOUNDLAND

Atlantic Ocean

*Gulf of
St. Lawrence*

← **Harp seals are
born here.**

MAGDALEN ISLANDS

Prince Edward Island

CANADA

NOVA SCOTIA

CANADA

UNITED
STATES

**This is the area
shown in the
big map.** ←

Loud helicopters arrive, waking the baby harp seal from a deep sleep. The baby's name is Harpo, and he is only ten days old.

Harpo sniffs the air and stares curiously at the noisy machines. Strange orange shapes merge and move across the ice toward him, black objects dangling from their necks. They call to each other and make funny noises. Most of them carry long sticks and thump the ice in front of them as they walk. The shapes come closer and closer, their feet crunch, crunch, crunching in the snow.

Harpo's mother suddenly dives through an air hole into the sea, leaving Harpo alone. All the older seals follow, though some of the young seal mothers stay with their pups. The baby seals cannot yet swim. Harpo lets out an alarmed cry that carries for miles.

Beneath the ice, Harpo's mother swims quickly, pushing herself along with her strong back flippers. When she is far enough away, she bobs up through an air hole to breathe and watch and wait.

In her memory, people were hunters who came out on the ice floe to kill the babies. They clubbed them and took the glossy white fur onto big boats, and went away again.

When she was a baby, she herself had been struck with a club. She had managed to escape, but it had taken months for the gash on her head to heal, and she still had a dreadful scar. Over the years she had watched helplessly while many of her own babies were killed by hunters. Would the same thing happen to Harpo?

The orange figures move closer toward the baby seals. Harpo's mother slips silently back into the sea. There is nothing she can do but hide in the water until the people go away. The black skin on her back, which forms the shape of a harp, is now invisible beneath the ice. It will be many years before Harpo develops a black harp shape like this on his back.

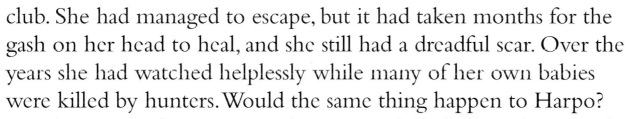

On the ice, Harpo loses interest in the orange shapes. He is hungry, scared, alone. When his mother does not return, he pushes himself through the snow toward one of the young seal mothers.

Maybe she will nurse him.

WHAM! Harpo feels the sting of a blow to his head. The young mother slaps him again with her flipper. Now he learns that other mothers will not nurse him. They have only enough milk for their own pups.

Turning, Harpo moves slowly across the ice. He is very hungry. He heads for the place where his mother had disappeared. The orange shapes are moving closer. Harpo buries his nose in the snow and shivers.

He has to find her.

Still in the water, Harpo's mother can stand it no longer. Raising her head from an air hole, she searches the ice for Harpo and for the hunters with their heavy clubs. The orange figures now raise black boxes to their eyes, pointing them toward the babies.

Hungry and frightened, Harpo wriggles across the
ice to an air hole. He peers into the dark water below.
Sure enough, some seals seem to be swimming down there.
Maybe his mother is there. Harpo leans way over.
SPLASH! He falls in.

He frantically beats the water with his flippers. Then he begins to spin, twirling around and around in the freezing water. He feels himself sinking. As the water closes over his head, Harpo catches sight of a bright orange shape looming over him.

A young girl, Sarah, has seen Harpo fall in. Now she kneels down beside the water. She knows that a frightened seal will scratch or bite anyone who tries to help it.

The young visitor reaches carefully and grabs Harpo by the back of his neck with her right hand. He is really heavy! Trembling, the baby seal tries with all his strength to get free, but Sarah holds him firmly. Then with her left hand, she takes Harpo's back flipper and pulls him out of the water.

A boy runs over shouting, "Is he okay?"

"Fine!" Sarah says. "Only a little frightened, because he's still too young to swim."

She sets Harpo gently down on the ice.

A man walks up and speaks to Sarah. His name is Brian. "There used to be a large fur trade here, you know. A lot of baby harp seals were killed, and the killing ended only when enough people stopped buying the fur. I guess they figured some other way to make coats and souvenirs for the tourists."

Sarah asks, "What made them stop wanting the fur?"

"I guess they learned to care more about these beautiful animals than about wearing fur," the man replies.

"I'm so glad," Sarah said.

"But there are a lot of people who want the hunt to start again," her new friend warned.

Harpo feels the ice under his flippers. He trembles. As the girl pets him a few times, his trembling stops. He is still hungry, but safe.

Harpo edges away from the people and wiggles under a shelf of overhanging ice. BOOM! A big chunk of ice falls down in front of him. He is trapped! He has backed too far into the small hollow, and the fallen chunk blocks his way out. Now his mother can never hear his cries. He is buried in a frozen cave.

Sarah sees what happened and rushes over. She punches and jabs the frozen chunk. It doesn't move. She grabs her walking stick and with all her strength stabs the ice until a small hole cracks open.

The baby seal huddles in the ice cave. For several minutes the girl scoops away ice and snow. Her hands inside her gloves are stinging with the cold. Finally, there is room to lift the baby seal out. Harpo is free!

Sarah smiles at the white furry seal who seems to be all whiskers, nose, and enormous dark eyes.

"Great job!" the boy shouts to his friend as an exhausted Harpo lays his head down on the snow and sleeps.

The visitors in the orange suits, black cameras dangling, return to the helicopters and climb aboard. The engines start and the machines take off. The seals close their eyes against the snow that is blown up by the whirling blades. Their thick blubber keeps them warm in the freezing wind.

Before long all is quiet again except for
the cries of the baby seals. Harpo sniffs and
sniffs the air, but cannot smell his mother.

Under the ice floe, Harpo's mother swims slowly and listens carefully. She can no longer hear the crunch of footsteps above her. Everything is silent except for the creak of the ice and the cries of the babies.

She speeds through the water with smooth strokes of her flippers. She knows Harpo will be very hungry by now.

Reaching an air hole,
she pulls herself onto the
ice with the long nails on
her front flippers.

Harpo is not there. Did the people kill him?
Has he been hurt? She begins a frantic search.

Lifting her head, she listens to the cries of the baby seals. One very loud cry seems familiar. She wriggles across the ice toward that sound.

She comes around an air hole,
and is suddenly beside her baby,
sniffing him. Harpo sniffs too.
It is his mother!

Harpo's mother rolls over, and Harpo begins to nurse. Warmth spreads through his body as he feeds on the rich milk. When he is full, Harpo falls asleep — warm, safe and, best of all, not hungry any more.

What Is a Harp Seal?

These photographs were taken in a nursery of harp seals on ice floes in the Gulf of St. Lawrence in northeast Canada.

Harp seal pups weighing around 15 to 20 pounds are born in late February or early March and are nursed approximately 12 to 14 days by their mothers. Their fur, slightly yellow at birth, quickly becomes bleached to snowy white from the sun.

A few days after their birth, the mothers leave the pups for short periods to swim. The mothers continue to watch their pups and feed them about every four hours.

As the pups grow, a thick layer of blubber forms around their bodies, providing them with food and insulation from the cold. By the time they are two weeks old, they will weigh from 66 to 100 pounds.

On the thirteenth or fourteenth day, the baby harp seals begin to moult and lose their baby fur. They are called "ragged-jackets" during this period.

The mothers leave then and head north toward the Arctic for the summer, starting a round trip journey of more than 3,000 miles (5,000 kilometers). The babies stay on the ice for three more weeks until the ice begins to break up and melt. During this time, the young seals are nourished by their own blubber.

The baby harp seals teach themselves to swim and later to fish. By this time they have completely shed their white coats and are called "beaters" because they beat the water when they learn to swim. They nuzzle each other for comfort. Ninety-eight percent will survive this period and swim northward like their mothers to the waters around Greenland. Each winter they will return to the Gulf of St. Lawrence, and after about five years, they will start their own families.

Seals live 30 to 35 years and are a spotted grey color. As the animals grow older, a black harp shape appears on their backs, which is why they are called harp seals.

Brian Davies, Patricia Arrigoni, and Fred Bruemmer at the Charlottetown Airport, Prince Edward Island, Canada, before flying out to the ice floes to see the baby harp seals.

Patricia Arrigoni
Author and Photographer

Patricia Arrigoni is a travel writer, author, columnist, and photographer. For several years, her columns and photographs were syndicated across the country by Gannett News Service, and she now contributes travel articles to Copley News Service. She has also written for other newspapers and magazines, including the *Chicago Tribune, National Geographic Traveler, International Travel News,* and *Far East Traveler.* Her guidebook on Marin County in Northern California, *Making the Most of Marin,* has been a continuous best seller since 1981.

Arrigoni has long been interested in marine mammals and served for years as a volunteer and board member for a natural science museum that housed injured seals. She also was co-founder of the internationally known Marine Mammal Center at Fort Cronkhite, California where all types of rescued sick and injured marine mammals are rehabilitated and released.

Harpo, the Baby Harp Seal is the outgrowth of her experiences visiting harp seals on the ice floes in the Gulf of St. Lawrence, Canada, for three consecutive years.

Patricia Arrigoni resides in the San Francisco Bay Area.

Brian Davies
Founder of the International Fund for Animal Welfare

Brian Davies is an author and animal advocate from Wales who has dedicated his life to stopping the slaughter of the baby harp seals. In 1969 he founded the International Fund for Animal Welfare, an organization that has over a million members. Davies now resides in Florida.

Fred Bruemmer
Photographer

Fred Bruemmer, an anthropologist and photographer, is famous for his studies of the Eskimos and wildlife. He is the author of 18 books, sold worldwide. He resides in Montreal, Canada.

David White
Photographer

David White is a freelance press and public relations photographer and the official photographer for the International Fund for Animal Welfare. He resides in Berkshire, England.

For information about IFAW, write:

International Fund for Animal Welfare
P. O. Box 193
Yarmouth Port, MA 02675 USA
Or telephone.: 800-932-4329

To participate in Seal Watch, contact
Natural Habitat Adventures at 800-543-8917.